This Walker book
belongs to:

To Victor

WALKER BOOKS
AND SUBSIDIARIES
LONDON · BOSTON · SYDNEY · AUCKLAND

First published 2015 by Walker Books Ltd, 87 Vauxhall Walk, London SE11 5HJ • This edition published 2016 for Scottish Book Trust
10 9 8 7 6 5 4 3 2 1 • © 2015 Mary Murphy • This book was hand-lettered • The moral rights of the author/illustrator have been asserted • Printed in China

Good Night Like This

Mary Murphy

Yawny
and dozy,
twitchy
and cosy.

Good night,
rabbits,
sleep tight...

Flitty and shiny,
flashy and
tiny.

Good night,
Fireflies,
sleep tight...

Quiet and strong,
all winter long.

Good night,
bears,
sleep tight...

Tickly
and feathery,
in any old
weathery.

Good night,
ducks,
sleep tight...

Snorey
and furry,
stretchy
and purry.

Good night, cats,
sleep tight...

Swoosh, swish,
make a
bedtime wish.

Good night, mice,
sleep tight...

Look! Everyone's tucked up
in bed – now it's your turn,
you sleepyhead.

So, good night,
you,
sleep tight...

Other books by Mary Murphy:

SAY HELLO LIKE THIS!
978-1-4063-5994-7

A KISS LIKE THIS
978-1-4063-4538-4

SLOW SNAIL
978-1-4063-3908-6

QUICK DUCK!
978-1-4063-3907-9

ARE YOU MY MUMMY?
978-1-4063-5378-5

MOUSE IS SMALL
978-1-4063-4828-6

CROCOPOTAMUS
978-1-4063-5789-9

UTTERLY LOVELY ONE
978-1-4063-3774-7

Praise for
Say Hello Like This!:

"A fun, interactive book to read aloud …
a guaranteed hit and a hoot"
INIS MAGAZINE

Praise for
A Kiss Like This:

"Sure to inspire lots of cuddles"
KIRKUS REVIEWS

Available from all good booksellers

www.walker.co.uk